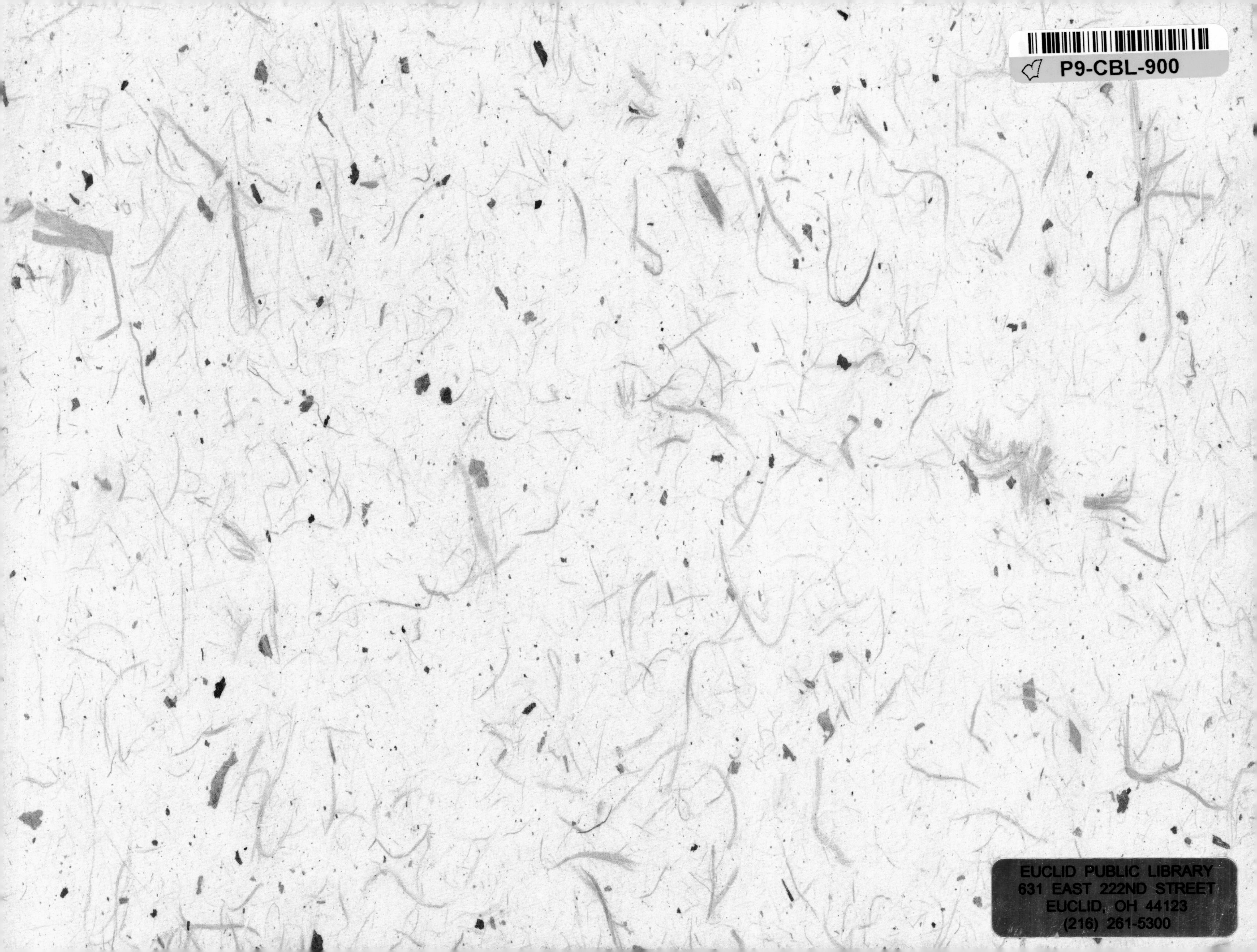
P9-CBL-900
EUCLID PUBLIC LIBRARY
631 EAST 222ND STREET
EUCLID, OH 44123
(216) 261-5300

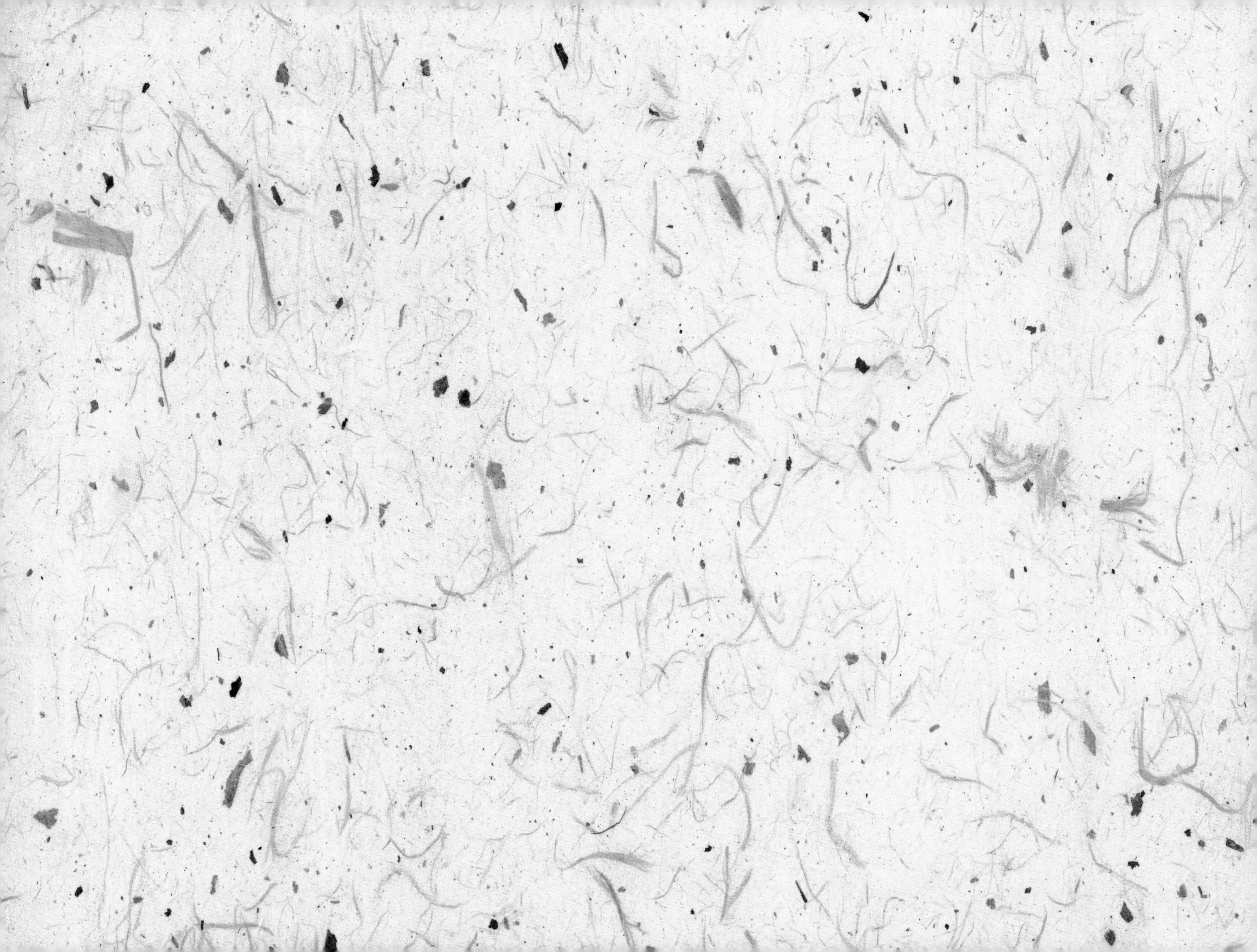

Just One More

by Wendi Silvano Illustrated by Ricardo Gamboa

all about kids publishing
SAN JOSE

All About Kids Publishing
6280 San Ignacio Ave., Suite C
San Jose, CA 95119
www.aakp.com

Editor: Lisa M. Tooker
Book Design: Libby Ellis

Printed in Hong Kong

For information about permission to reproduce
any selection from this book, write to:
All About Kids Publishing
6280 San Ignacio Ave., Suite C
San Jose, CA 95119
www.aakp.com

Library of Congress Card Number: 2001094290
ISBN: 0-9700863-7-7

To Eddy and our little angels, Nicole, Madison, Natalie, Liliana and Keaton
—Wendi Silvano

For my sweet nieces and nephews, and with a special thanks to my parents, Carlos and Socorro
—Ricardo Gamboa

The rickety old bus came bouncing down the dirt road from high up in the Andes Mountains.

It stopped, and Hector climbed on. The bus was full. The seats were full. The aisle was full. There were people and bags and bundles and boxes everywhere. The driver yelled to the passengers, "Move back!"

Hector wiggled into the space behind the driver's seat, and the bus pulled out.

Just down the road the bus stopped again. Hector watched, while a twisted-looking old man swayed and swerved his way up the steps, holding a bottle of soda pop that wobbled and bobbled in his hand.

Hector looked around.

"There's no more room, this bus is packed," said Hector, "we are piled and stacked up to the roof and out the door." But the bus driver hollered, "Just one more!"

The old man bumped and jostled his way to the back of the bus. He took a big gulp of his soda, leaned his head back on the seat and fell asleep. The bus drove on.

The bus stopped again. Up the steps bounced a short, pudgy woman with a crinkly smile. In her hand she carried a mesh bag, chock-full of chickens. Hector looked at the woman. He looked at the chickens.

"There's no more room, this bus is packed," said Hector, "we are piled and stacked up to the roof and out the door." But the driver hollered, "Just one more!"

The chickens cackled and clucked, as the woman squished those around her and squeezed her way into the aisle. The bus drove on.

Hardly a minute later the bus stopped again. A dainty young woman, wearing a colorful shawl, climbed aboard with a baby strapped on her back. Hector smiled at the baby. The baby smiled back.

Then Hector looked around and frowned.

"There's no more room, this bus is packed," said Hector, "we are piled and stacked up to the roof and out the door." But the driver hollered, "Just one more!"

A man stood up and gave the woman his seat. She carefully sat down, and the man wrestled himself a spot among the crunched crowd.

The baby's head bobbed up and down in the shawl, while the chickens cackled and clucked, and the twisted old man snored up a storm. The bus drove on.

Just down the road the bus stopped again. Hector stared at the grunting pig, squiggling in the arms of a roly-poly woman, who was wiggling her way up the steps. Hector rolled his eyes.

"There's no more room, this bus is packed," said Hector, "we are piled and stacked up to the roof and out the door." But the driver hollered, "Just one more!"

The woman and the pig smooshed themselves into the aisle. The pig squealed, while the chickens clucked and the baby fussed and the old man snored. It was getting louder on the bus! The aisle was jammed! But the bus drove on.

Then the bus stopped again. Hector's eyes bulged as a young boy stepped aboard, pulling behind him a woolly, white llama. "Oh, no!" said Hector.

"There's no more room, this bus is packed," said Hector, "we are piled and stacked up to the roof and out the door." But the driver hollered, "Just one more!"

The boy and his llama pressed their way to the top of the stairs, and the bus drove on.

The bus clamored with sounds of squealing and cackling, snoring and crying, jiggling and jostling, as it bumped on down the road.

The bus pulled over again. In came a bundle of hay that was tied on the back of an odd-looking man, who was pushing his way up the steps. The man looked around. Hector looked around.

"There's no more room, this bus is packed," said Hector, "we are piled and stacked up to the roof and out the door." But the driver hollered, "Just one more!"

The man tried to squeeze in, but could not get any farther than the doorway. He turned around and plopped down on the middle step. The llama began munching and crunching the delicious hay he found stuffed in front of his face. The bus drove on.

Again the bus came to a stop. Five rowdy schoolboys clambered aboard with their books. Hector looked at the boys, then he looked around. He sighed.

"There's no more room, this bus is packed," said Hector, "we are piled and stacked up to the roof and out the door." But the driver hollered, "Just five more!"

The boys squished, they squeezed, they squiggled, they squirmed; but they just could not get even one leg past the jammed passengers.

They hung in the doorway, clutching the door, the rail and each other, to keep from falling out. The bus drove on.

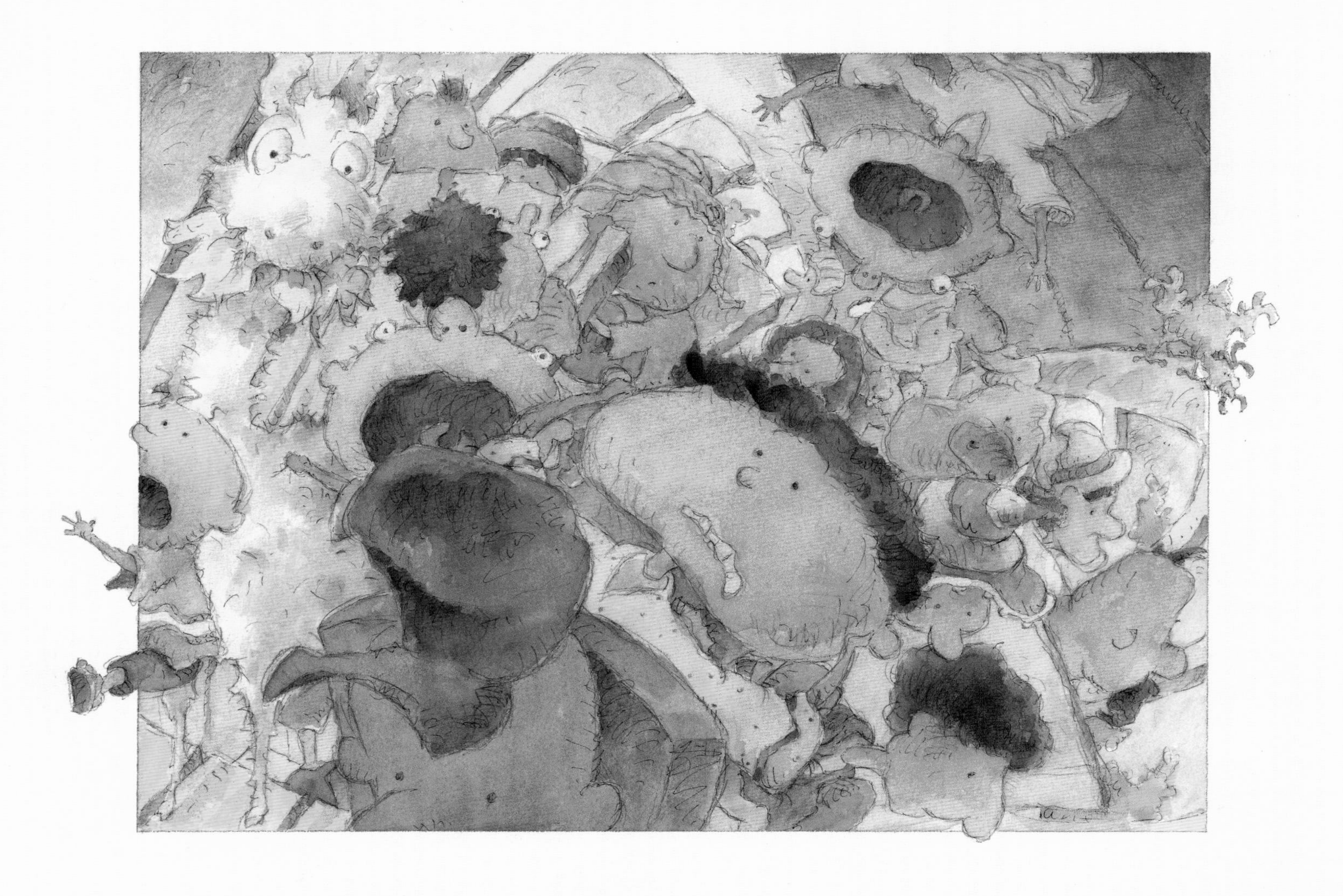

The bus swayed and bounced as it made its way down the rocky road. Hector could hear the chickens cackling, the baby fussing, the old man snoring, the pig squealing, the llama munching and the five school boys hollering, each time the bus went over a bump. The noise was awful! The smell was worse! Hector wanted off, but he couldn't move an inch.

"THERE'S NO MORE ROOM, THIS BUS IS PACKED," yelled Hector, "WE ARE PILED AND STACKED UP TO THE ROOF AND OUT THE DOOR." The driver hollered, "OKAY, NO MORE!"

The bus continued on for several minutes. Then, just as it was rounding a sharp curve, the old man at the back let out an enormous, thunderous...

It **startled** the baby,

who **screamed**
at the pig,

who **jumped**
onto the llama,

who **kicked**
the driver,

who **lost**
the wheel,

and the bus went
crashing down into
a ditch and stopped,
with a THUD!

One by one the passengers crawled, climbed and scrambled their way off the bus and onto the road. Each one headed out the door with boxes, bundles, books, a baby, chickens, a pig, and a llama.

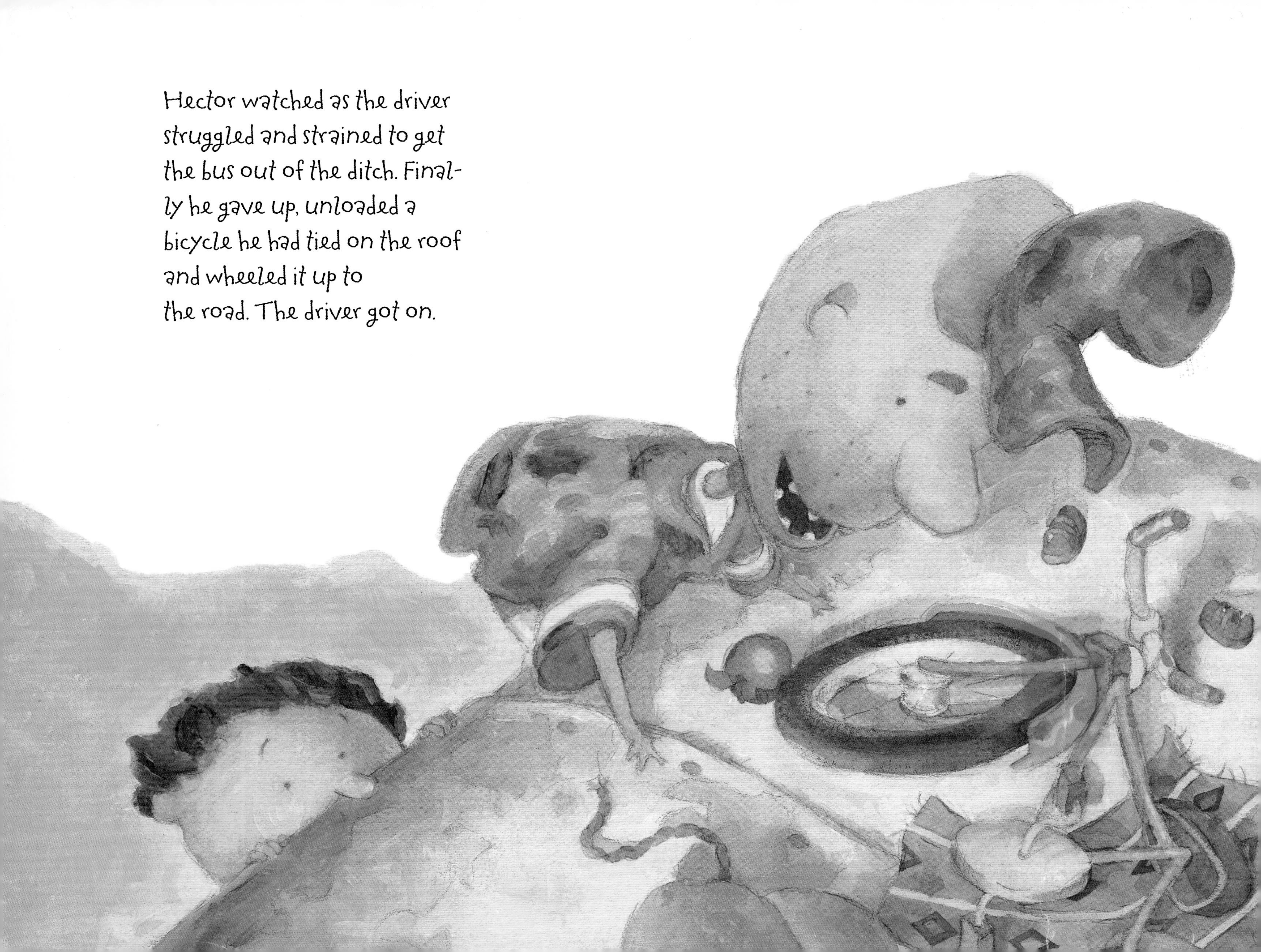

Hector watched as the driver struggled and strained to get the bus out of the ditch. Finally he gave up, unloaded a bicycle he had tied on the roof and wheeled it up to the road. The driver got on.

Hector looked at the bicycle. Then he looked at the driver and sheepishly asked, "Just one more?"

With a chuckle and a grin, the driver answered back, "Just one more."

Hector climbed on the back and together they rode off down the bumpy road towards home.

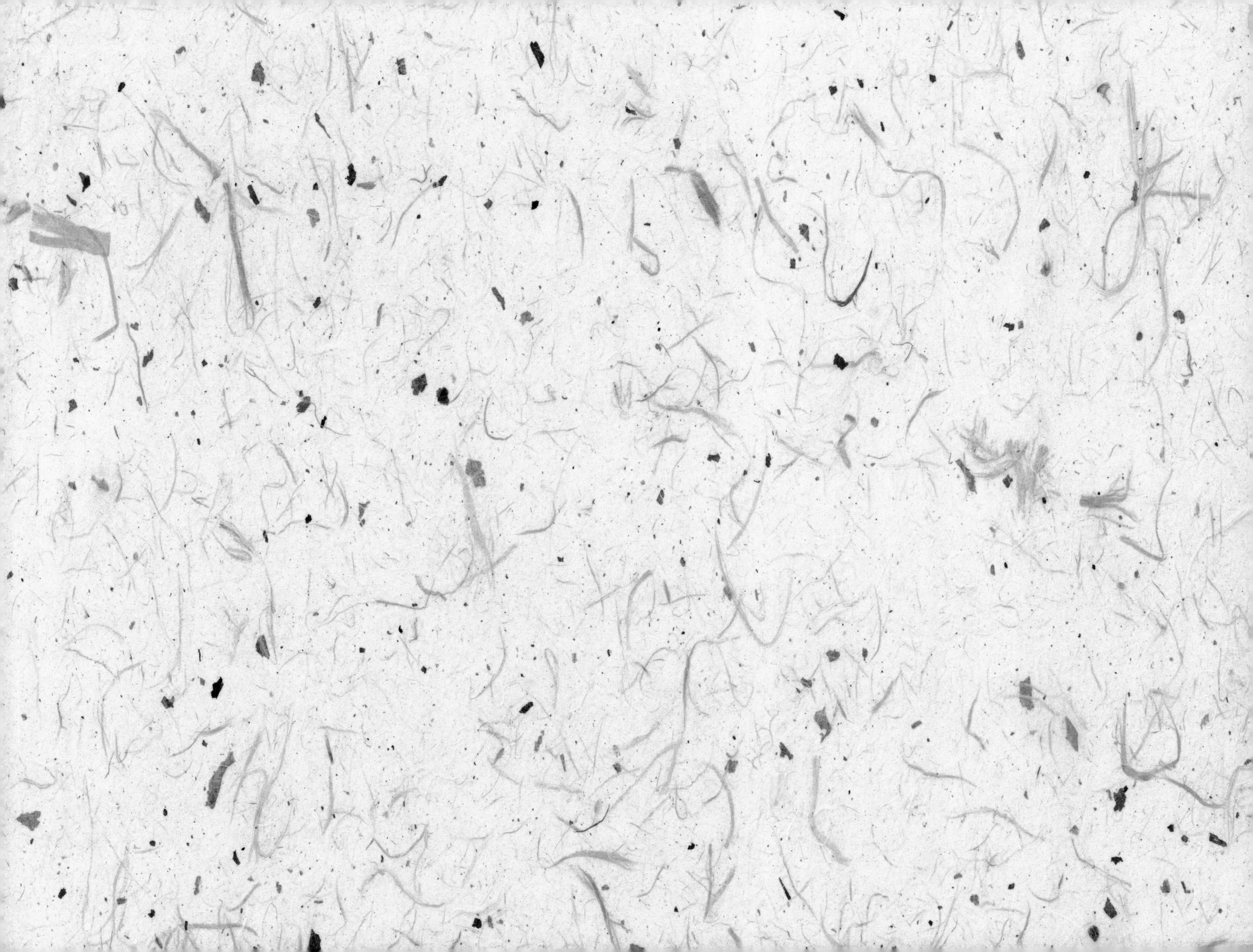

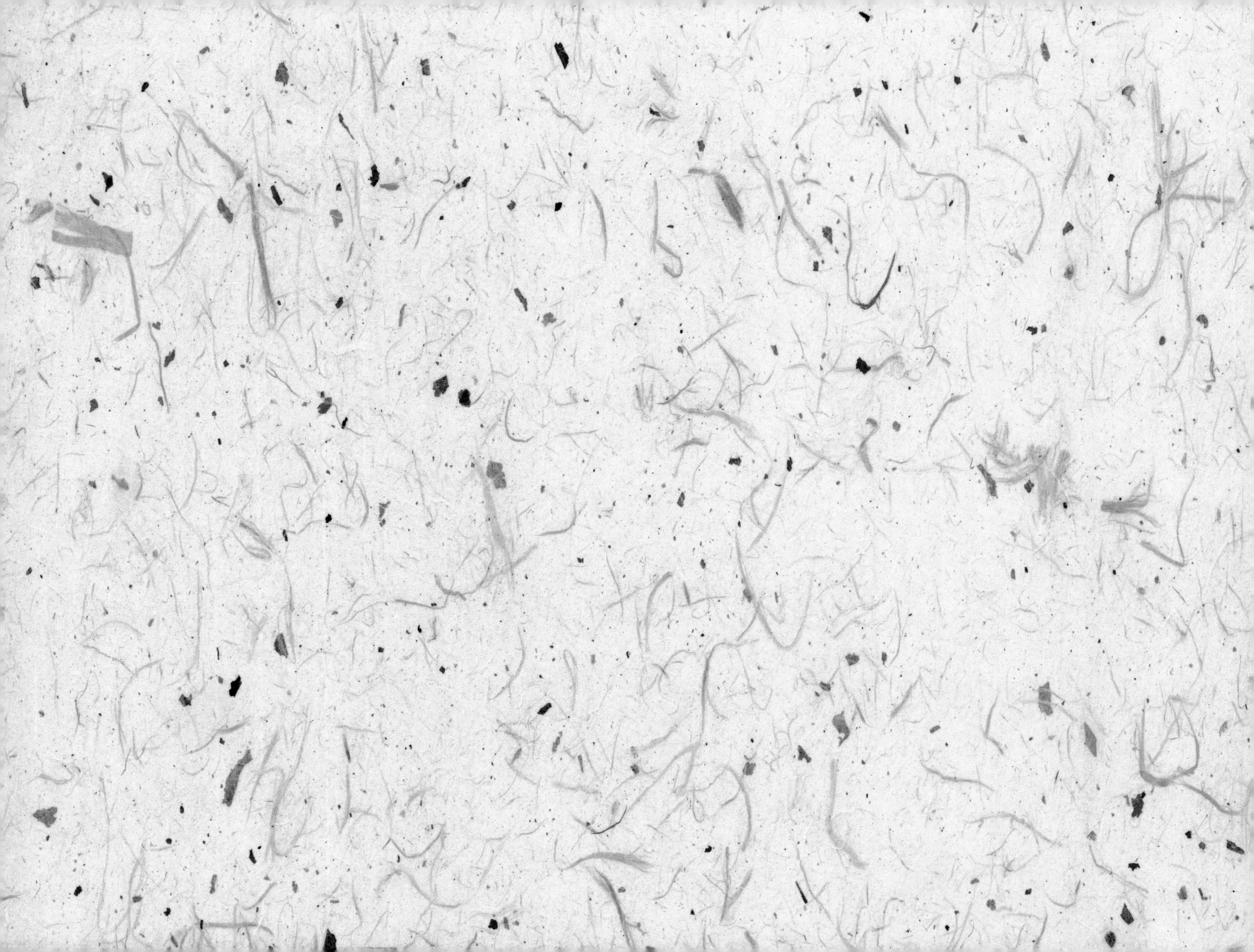